PEOPLES OF THE WORLD

Roma Trundle

Illustrated by Bob Hersey, Rob McCaig and Joseph McEwan

Designed by Graham Round

Edited by Lisa Watts

Contents

Consultant editor: Barry Dufour, Fellow of the Royal Anthropological Institute and Lecturer in Education, School of Education, University of Leicester, England.
Research assistant: Jane Chisholm
Additional designs by Anna Barnard

© Usborne Publishing Ltd 1990, 1978. First published in 1978 by Usborne Publishing Ltd, Usborne House, 83-85 Saffron Hill, London EC1N 8RT, England. Printed in Belgium

The name Usborne and the device 🜲 are Trade Marks of Usborne Publishing Ltd.

Peoples and their countries

There are over 150 countries in the world. Some of them are huge, with hundreds of millions of people, while others are as small as cities with populations of only a few thousand.

People in different countries have their own customs, traditions, languages and beliefs. Some of the large countries have lots of different peoples, each with their own customs and languages.

1 What is a country?

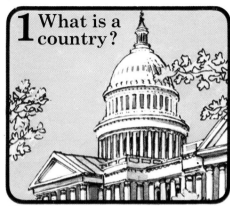

Each country has its government which rules the people. This picture shows Capitol Hill in Washington, U.S.A. where the American Government, called the Congress, meets.

2

Every country has a flag and most have a national anthem. The Union Jack, seen here on the Tower of London, is the flag of the United Kingdom.

3

Countries have their own money and stamps which can usually be used only within their boundaries. Coins, notes and stamps often have pictures of famous people or places on them.

4

People in different countries usually speak different languages. In some countries, several languages are spoken and used on signposts like this one in the Sahara Desert in Mali.

5

In Japan, it is a custom for people to greet each other by bowing. People in other countries have their own special customs too, such as shaking hands.

Travelling abroad

To travel to another country you need a travel document called a passport. This shows your nationality, and the country you come from.

You need special permission to enter some countries. In these cases, you must have a visa stamped in your passport by the country's embassy.

At the boundaries between countries there are barriers across the roads. Here the frontier police examine your passport and watch out for smugglers.

Before you can buy anything in another country, you have to get your money changed at a bank or *bureau de change*.

Flags

The Union Jack, flag of the United Kingdom, is a combination of the red cross of St George, white cross of St Andrew and red cross of St Patrick.

The Australian flag shows the Southern Cross, a group of stars which can be seen in the Australian sky.

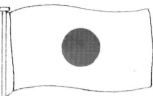

The red circle on the Japanese flag represents the sun and the name Japan means "land of the rising sun" in Japanese.

The red maple tree leaf on the Canadian flag is the symbol of Canada. This flag was first used in 1965.

In 1991, the old pre-revolutionary blue and white flag of Russia was restored. It replaced the communist flag, which was first used in 1917.

The flag of the U.S.A. has 50 stars, one for each of the states. The 13 stripes represent the 13 original states.

On the flag of Saudi Arabia are the words "There is no god but God and Muhammad is his Prophet", written in Arabic.

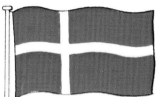

The Danish flag is the oldest in the world. It has been used for over 600 years.

Tribal peoples

In some parts of the world there are groups, or tribes of people whose customs and traditions are different from those of the country they live in. These peoples often have their own leaders, but they still have to obey the laws of the country they live in. Nowadays many of these people are moving to live in towns and are giving up their traditional ways of life.

The Bedouin are a people who live by herding camels and sheep in the Arabian desert. Nowadays, many of them are settling to live in the towns.

The Masai live in Kenya and Tanzania, in East Africa. They have their own language and live mainly by herding cattle.

Many different tribal peoples live in the Xingu National Park, a reservation in the Amazon forest, in South America.

Rich and poor countries

The rich countries are those which have lots of factories or large quantities of a natural product such as oil. Countries where most people work in factories or offices are called industrialized countries.

In the poorer countries most people still work on the land as farmers. They do not have many factories and often grow crops such as sugar, coffee or cotton to sell to the rich countries.

Country collections

There are lots of ways of making a country collection. You could collect everything you can find about one country, such as fruit and food wrappers, coins, stamps, postcards and pictures from travel brochures. Or you could limit your collection to one topic, such as stamps, or pictures of national costumes, flags or football players and collect these for lots of different countries.

Peoples' ancestors

Many millions of years ago, our ancestors were monkey-like creatures living in the trees. Like all other animals, people have slowly developed and changed to become as they are today.

Everyone in the world belongs to the same biological group, or species. This group is called *Homo sapiens*, which is Latin for "wise man".

These monkey-like creatures lived about 14 million years ago and are the ancestors of people. There were no people on Earth then.

The first people lived about three million years ago. They ate grubs and berries and hunted for animals which they killed with rocks and sticks.

Gradually, our early ancestors learned how to hunt larger animals. They made tools for cutting meat by chipping stones to give them sharp edges.

Tent made of animal skins.

For hundreds of thousands of years, people lived by hunting animals and collecting fruits to eat. There were no towns or villages and they lived in caves, or in huts built from sticks and animal skins or grass.

Chipping a rock to make a stone tool.

They were skilled at making sharp tools from stones, or from the bones or antlers of animals. They had not yet discovered how to weave cloth or to sew and their clothes were made from animal skins.

People first discovered they could grow food by planting seeds about 11,000 years ago. They settled near their farmland and built villages.

The villages gradually grew into towns. People learned how to weave and make pottery and traded things they made with people from other towns.

Races of people

There are four main races of people living in the world today, though all of them belong to the same group, or species of mankind: *Homo sapiens.*

Each race has its own special characteristics, such as the narrow eyes of the Mongoloid race, or the black skin of Negroes. Scientists think that early people in different parts of the world gradually developed characteristics that helped them to survive.

This Chinese boy belongs to the Mongoloid race.

Aboriginal boy from Australia belongs to the Australoid race.

This man from South Africa belongs to the Negroid race.

This Swiss girl belongs to the Caucasoid race.

Black skin protects people from the sun in very hot, wet places and the narrow eyes of Mongoloid people are a protection against extreme cold. Today racial differences are less important, because clothes, houses, heating and prepared foods enable people of any race to survive almost anywhere.

Tools

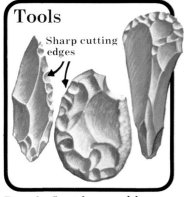

Sharp cutting edges

People first learned how to make stone tools about 2½ million years ago. Later as they became more skilful they made sharp stone scrapers and knives.

Metals

Blowing on fire to make it hotter.

Metal tools were first made over 5,000 years ago. They lasted longer and were easier to make than stone tools. Copper and gold were used first.

Cooking

Cooking was probably learned by accident when meat fell into the fire. It made it tastier and easier to chew. People roasted food on hot stones.

Clothes

Bone needles were invented 40,000 years ago. They were used for sewing skins together with leather strips, and for decorating them with shells and teeth.

Beliefs

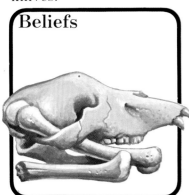

This cave bear's skull with a leg bone through it was found in a cave where early people lived. They probably believed it would make magic.

Painting

People discovered how to paint with powdered coloured rocks, mixed with animal fat. Their brushes were made of animal hair.

Pottery

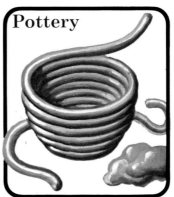

The Stone Age farmers were the first people to discover how to make pottery by baking clay in a fire. They made pots from coils of clay.

Writing

The marks on this piece of clay are some of the first writing. It was done by people called the Sumerians who lived about 5,000 years ago.

5

Language and writing

Over 4,000 languages are spoken in the world today. In some countries there are several languages and in India there are over 800. Sometimes people in one country speak different versions, or dialects of the same language. Some languages, such as English and Spanish, are spoken in many different parts of the world*

Here are six children from different countries speaking in their own languages.

Hej, jag heter, Margareta.

This is Swedish. It is pronounced "Hay, yag heer-ta Mar-gar-ret-a" and means "Hello, my name is Margareta".

Hola, me llamo Pablo.

This is Spanish. It is pronounced "O-la, may ya-mo Pablo" and means "Hello, my name is Pablo".

ЗДРАВСТВУЙТЕ, МЕНЯ ЗОВУТ САША

This is Russian. It is pronounced "Is-drast-vooey-ti-ey men-yah zov-wot Sarsha" and means "Hello, my name is Sarsha"

Language families

People who study languages have discovered that many of them are related and can be grouped together into language families. This chart shows some of the languages in the Indo-European family. There are eight main groups in this language family. Two of the groups: Germanic and Romance, and some of the languages in them, are shown here.

INDO-EUROPEAN LANGUAGE FAMILY About half the world's peoples speak a language from this family.	GERMANIC The languages in this group developed from a language spoken long ago.	GERMAN	GUTEN MORGEN
		ENGLISH	GOOD MORNING
		DUTCH	GOEDE MORGEN
		SWEDISH	GOD MORGON
		NORWEGIAN	GOD MORGEN
	ROMANCE The languages in this group all developed from Latin. The words shown here mean "man" in English.	ITALIAN	UOMO
		SPANISH	HOMBRE
		FRENCH	HOMME
		PORTUGUESE	HOMEM
		ROMANIAN	OM

All the languages in a family developed from the same parent language. As groups of people spread out across the world, they took their language with them. They began to pronounce words in a slightly different way from their ancestors, and had to find new words for foreign things, so gradually their language changed.

Writing

An alphabet is a set of symbols which stand for the sounds which make words. There are many different alphabets and ways of writing. Arabic is written from right to left, and Chinese does not have an alphabet at all. Instead it uses "characters" to stand for words or parts of words.

1 Latin or Roman alphabet

A B C D E
F G H I J K
L M N O P
Q R S T U
V W X Y Z

Most West European languages use this alphabet. Some of them add signs to the letters, e.g. ö, to show how they should be pronounced.

2 Arabic alphabet

ب ت ث ج ح
خ د ذ ر ز س
ش ص ض ط ظ
ع غ ف ق ك ل
م ن هـ و ي

Arabic is the second most widely used alphabet. Other languages such as Persian and Urdu (used in Pakistan) are also written in it.

3 Picture signs / Modern Chinese characters

Man 大 尺 人
Tree 朮 朮 木
Bird 鳥 鳥 鳥

Modern Chinese characters developed from picture signs. They are now written from left to right, but used to be written in columns down the page.

The chart on pages 28-31 shows which languages people speak.

Numbers

European	Arab	Chinese
1	١	一
2	٢	二
3	٣	三
4	٤	四
5	٥	五

This is Arabic. It is pronounced "Mar-huba, iss-mee Layla" and means "Hello, my name is Layla".

This is Hindi which is spoken in India. It is pronounced "Nam-as-tay, mera naam Rah-day Shaam hi" and means "Hello, my name is Rahday Shaam".

This is Chinese. It is pronounced "Nee how, wah ming tzer Tsee-ow Hoong" and means "Hello, my name is Tseeow Hoong".

The numbers used in western Europe are called Arabic numerals and developed from numbers used by the Arabs 1,000 years ago. Chinese and some other languages have their own signs for numbers.

Greek

Greek was the first European language to have a written form. The word "alphabet" comes from the names of the first two Greek letters: *alpha* and *beta*.

African languages

This man is reading a newspaper written in Swahili, the main East African language. Over 1,000 languages are spoken in Africa. Some have no written form.

India

Hindi, which this girl is learning to read, is one of the languages of India. Many Indians speak Hindustani, a mixture of Hindi and another language called Urdu.

South America

PORTUGUESE
SPANISH
AMERICAN INDIAN

Many South American countries used to be ruled by Spain or Portugal, so Spanish and Portuguese are spoken there. American Indian languages are also spoken.

Arabic

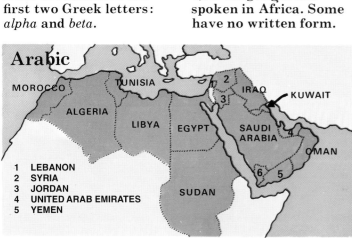

MOROCCO
TUNISIA
ALGERIA
LIBYA
EGYPT
IRAQ
KUWAIT
SAUDI ARABIA
OMAN
SUDAN

1 LEBANON
2 SYRIA
3 JORDAN
4 UNITED ARAB EMIRATES
5 YEMEN

Arabic is the official language of all these countries. It spread out across these areas long ago, when followers of the Prophet Muhammad converted the people to their religion, Islam. The Islamic holy book, the Koran, is written in Arabic.

Chinese

There are lots of Chinese dialects, but everyone can understand these posters as they all use the same written language. The main dialect is Mandarin.

Written Chinese has over 40,000 different characters. Children at school need learn only about 3,000 of them for everyday use.

Money

Each country has its own money called its currency.*Some have the same name for their currency—more than 20 countries use "dollars"—but they all have different values.

The foreign exchange rate decides how much of another country's currency you can buy with your money. This rate often varies from day to day.

Notes and coins

Indian 100 rupee note. Writing is in eight Indian languages and English.

Greek 50 drachma note which shows the head of Helen of Troy, daughter of an ancient Greek god.

2 drachma piece

Iranian 50 rial note and 5 and 10 rial coins. Note shows ancient temple of Shiraz and antelope, old symbol of Iran.

Spanish 100 peseta note with picture of a Spanish composer.

1 Shops and shopping

This is a market called a *souk* in Jerusalem. There are no fixed prices and the stallkeeper and shopper argue about how much the goods are worth until they can agree a price.

In shops like this French greengrocer's the prices are fixed and shoppers do not usually bargain for a lower price.

This is an open-air market in Peru. Women bring food they have grown, but do not need, to sell to other villagers.

8
* *The chart on pages 28-31 shows what each country's currency is.*

◄ Japanese 1,000 yen note with picture of the Bank of Tokyo. Five yen coin with hole in it.

Malaysian sens. Picture on coin shows parliament building in Kuala Lumpur and Muslim crescent. ►

Money collection

Sometimes, you find foreign money in your change, or you can ask people travelling abroad to save you some. You can also buy coins from dealers.

You could collect coins which have pictures of ships, animals or famous people, or according to the country they come from.

You could also make a collection of your own country's money, looking out for old or unusual coins.

Austrian 50 schilling note and 10 schilling piece, which shows old Austrian head-dress. ▼

Russian 5 rouble note showing one of the towers of the Kremlin, the government building. ►

American dollar bill shows George Washington, the first president of the U.S.A. Also 25 and 5 cent coins.

Australian 20 cent piece with picture of duck-billed platypus. One cent piece shows a possum. ▼

3

Most big cities in the world have supermarkets which sell tinned and packaged foods. In America they stay open late nearly every night.

Living without money

Bushmen, who live in the Kalahari desert in Africa, use very little money. They hunt animals for food, build their own houses and make clothes from animal skins. Some are now beginning to work on farms for wages.

These people live and work on an Israeli kibbutz. They are given food and houses, and a little money for luxuries.

5

These women in a village in Iran are swopping a sack of grain for a carpet they have woven. Exchanging things like this is called bartering.

Money changers

This shopkeeper in Oman earns his living by buying and selling foreign currencies to tradesmen and travellers.

Storing wealth

The heavy gold earrings worn by this young Fulani girl from Africa, are her family's wealth. If they need money, they will sell some of the gold.

Unusual money

In this desert market in Ethiopia, people are paying for the things they need with bars of salt, which they use like money.

Food and cooking

In many countries, people eat very little meat. They have one main kind of filling food and eat it with sauces made with vegetables, spices or herbs. In Asia and the Middle East, the filling food is rice, in Africa it is maize, millet or white vegetables called yams. Potatoes are eaten in Europe and also in South America where they first came from. Everywhere people use flour made from wheat or other kinds of grain to make bread.

China

This family is eating steamed rice or noodles with vegetables and eggs or fish. Sometimes they flavour it with soya bean sauce. The Chinese do not eat much meat.

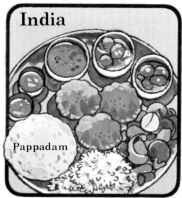

India

Pappadam

This is a special meal from western India. In the little bowls are rice, lentils, vegetable curry and crisps called pappadams. The curry is spicy but not always hot.

West Africa

Kitchen where food is cooked over a fire.

Millet

Forbidden foods

Some people do not eat certain foods because their religions forbid them. Hindus will not eat beef as cows are thought to be sacred and some do not eat any meat, fish or eggs as they are not supposed to kill animals. Muslims think pigs are unclean and do not eat pork. Jews have many rules and the foods which they may eat are called "kosher" foods.

Italy

This is a spaghetti-making machine. Spaghetti is a type of pasta made from wheat flour. It is cooked in different ways with meat, tomatoes, cheese or fish.

Germany

Many different kinds of sausages and smoked meats are eaten with warm, filling soups, pickled vegetables and rye bread called pumpernickel.

Cooking

In many parts of the world, outside the cities, people do not have gas or electric stoves. They cook over open fires or in clay ovens.

Cooking makes some foods tastier and easier to chew and digest. It also kills germs in the food. Cooked food usually keeps longer without going bad.

Before she can start cooking, this Indian woman has to light a wood fire. She cooks the food in shallow metal pans over the fire.

Women in a village in Cyprus share this clay oven for baking bread and pies. Most have stoves at home, but no ovens.

People who live in tents often barbeque their food on sticks. They have few pans to pack when they move camp.

Tall tower called a granary where grain is stored to keep it dry and away from rats.

Women work with their babies strapped to their backs.

Bowl made from dried skin of a fruit called a gourd.

In many African countries people grow a grain called millet. These village women from Upper Volta are pounding it to make a coarse flour.

They make a kind of porridge from the millet flour and eat it with vegetables and a peppery sauce. Meat is eaten only on special occasions.

Tunisia

This Tunisian family are eating a bowl of cous-cous. This is coarsely ground wheat, boiled and eaten with a vegetable or meat sauce.

Peru

This woman is making special pancakes, called tortillas, and filling them with potato spiced with hot peppers and lemon for her family's lunch.

The hungry world

Half the people in the world do not have enough to eat and millions die every year from starvation. Floods and droughts, poverty and wars prevent people in the developing countries from getting enough to eat. In richer countries people suffer diseases caused by eating too much rich or processed food.

Recipe for an Indian drink

To make this Indian drink, called *lassi*, you need a pot of plain yogurt, cold water, sugar, vanilla essence and a screw-topped container.

Put the yogurt into the container, then fill the yogurt pot with cold water and pour it in too. Add a teaspoonful of sugar and about 3 drops of vanilla essence. Screw on the top of the container and shake the mixture well. It tastes best chilled or with ice.

To make strawberry *lassi*, use strawberry flavoured yogurt and leave out the sugar and vanilla. You could use other flavours of yogurt too.

Milk and cheese

1

This is a dairy in Denmark. Huge herds of cows are milked quickly by machines to supply city people with milk.

2

People use the milk of lots of different animals such as sheep, goats, llamas and camels. This woman is milking a yak.

3

Milk keeps much longer if it is made into butter, cheese or yoghurt. This Bedouin woman is making butter in a goatskin.

4

These Swiss cheese makers are draining the "whey" from the solid milk "curds" which will be put in a mould to make a cheese called Emmental.

Gruyère from Switzerland

Brie from France

Manchego from Spain

Feta from Greece

Edam from Holland

Stilton from England

These are some cheeses from countries in Europe.

Clothes

Traditional clothes are still worn in many parts of the world. These clothes are suited to the climate and do not change with fashion. Loose, flowing clothes, such as saris and sarongs, are cool to wear. Thick layers of fur or padded felt clothes help keep people warm. It is usually the women who still dress in the traditional way. Men and young people, especially in cities, are now buying western-styled clothes.

1 Clothes for hot countries

Saris, which are worn by Indian women, are 6m lengths of silk or cotton cloth. Under their saris, they wear petticoats and short blouses.

2

Men and women in South-East Asia wear sarongs. These are lengths of cotton cloth which they wrap round their waists and wear with shirts or embroidered blouses.

Cold weather clothes

High in the Himalayan mountains, where the winters are bitterly cold, peoples' clothes are large and loose so they can wear lots of layers underneath. They are made of fur or thick felt and are often padded for extra warmth. The long, wide sleeves roll down to cover their hands, and ear-flaps protect their ears.

Hats and head-dresses

The light, straw, cone-shaped hats worn in South-East Asia, protect people from the sun and rain but are cool to wear.

A turban, like this man from Afghanistan is wearing, is a long piece of cloth wrapped round and round the head.

Arab men's head-dresses are plain white or have red or black patterns. The cloth is held on with a thick cord.

Village women in Bolivia wear felt bowler hats. These were first worn 50 years ago and were copied from Europeans.

3

People who live in deserts wear thin loose clothes to keep cool. This Tuareg tribesman from the Sahara covers his face and head too, for protection against the burning sun and blowing sand.

4

Women in many African countries wear brightly coloured cloths which they wrap round themselves. Some women wear western-style dresses made from this material.

5

Some of the tribal peoples who live in hot, rainy jungles wear only waistbands. They often rub coloured plant juices on to their skins to keep off insects.

1 Special clothes

In some Muslim countries women have to cover themselves from head to foot before going out. These Arab women from the Yemen wear long black robes and face masks.

2

Policemen, like this French *gendarme*, and soldiers, nurses and people in many other jobs, wear special uniforms so that they can be recognized.

3

The coloured head-dresses of these Kirghiz women from Russia have special meanings. Married women wear red and unmarried girls wear white.

4

The cross-stitch embroidery on this Arab woman's dress shows which town she comes from. Women from different towns have different embroidery.

Fashion

Elderly Japanese women still wear their traditional kimonos but younger girls wear modern fashion clothes. Fashion trends are much the same all over the world.

National costume

Sporran

Tartan kilt

This Scotsman is wearing his national costume. Most European countries have national costumes but they are worn only on special occasions or for tourists.

Ideas for dressing up

SARONG
1. SHEET OR MATERIAL ABOUT 2m LONG — SEW OR SAFETY PIN EDGES
2. FOLD ACROSS STOMACH AND TUCK IN AT WAIST — HOLD HERE
3. FOLD OTHER SIDE OVER — SAFETY PIN

SARI
1. LONG BIT OF MATERIAL eg. OLD SHEET TORN IN HALF LENGTH WAYS WITH ENDS SEWN TOGETHER — TUCK EDGE INTO PANTS
2. BRING MATERIAL IN FRONT OF YOU AND FOLD TO MAKE 4 BIG PLEATS — TUCK INTO PANTS
3. WIND MATERIAL BEHIND YOU, THEN UP OVER YOUR LEFT SHOULDER
4.

TURBAN
1. LONG SCARF OR BIT OF OLD SHEET
2. WIND ENDS ROUND FRONT OF HEAD
3. TUCK ENDS IN AT BACK

Hair, jewellery and make-up

People arrange their hair, paint their faces and wear jewellery to make themselves more attractive to others. People from different parts of the world have very different styles of decorating themselves. What some people think beautiful, others, with different traditions, may find very ugly. Women usually dress themselves up more than men, but among some tribal peoples, the men often spend hours decorating themselves.

The silver bands and coins worn by this woman from Laos are her family's savings and show how rich they are.

Jewellery

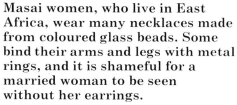

This Amazon jungle woman wears seeds and monkey's teeth. People often make jewellery from things they find.

Indian women sometimes wear rings in their noses. This shows that they are married.

Sometimes jewellery shows a person's religion. This Christian girl wears a cross.

Masai women, who live in East Africa, wear many necklaces made from coloured glass beads. Some bind their arms and legs with metal rings, and it is shameful for a married woman to be seen without her earrings.

Hair and hairstyles

People of different races have different types of hair. You can see the three main types below.

People of the Caucasoid race have straight or wavy hair. It may be blond, brown, reddish-brown or black.

Mongoloid people have thick, straight, black hair, and very little hair on their faces or bodies.

Negroes have dark, tightly curled hair. This probably developed as a protection against the hot sun.

In India, people think it is unfeminine for women to have short hair. They often wear it in long plaits. Young women are now breaking with this tradition and cutting their hair.

Make-up and body paint

Since prehistoric times people have painted and decorated their bodies. Over 5,000 years ago the Egyptians used eye make-up called kohl, made from a powdered rock. Kohl is still used in India and the Middle East.

Women all over the world use make-up. Modern make-up is made from chemical dyes and plant and animal oils.

This woman from the jungle in Peru paints her face with vegetable dyes. The patterns show which tribe she comes from.

At festival time, Huichol women from Mexico stick petals on their faces with lipstick so the gods know they want children.

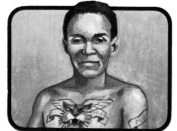

Sailors learned how to tattoo from Pacific islanders. The pattern is pricked into the skin and colour is rubbed in.

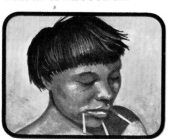

Since childhood, this woman from the Amazon jungle has worn little bits of wood stuck through her lips.

Hair plastered with beeswax and dusted with colour.

Mirror

Paint made from powdered rocks.

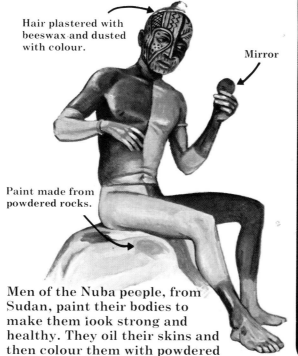

Men of the Nuba people, from Sudan, paint their bodies to make them look strong and healthy. They oil their skins and then colour them with powdered red or yellow rocks, black ashes or crushed white shells.

How to paint your face

Here are some Nuba face patterns you could try out. You can buy face paints at toy shops or theatre suppliers, or you could use old make-up. Use cold cream to remove your face paint.

RED LIPSTICK OR FACE PAINT

YELLOW AND BLACK FACE PAINT

"RED FOREST MONKEY"   "MASKED BIRD"

BLACK OR YELLOW FACE PAINT

TALCUM POWDER

"COW"   "ANTELOPE"

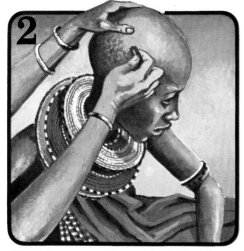

2

Masai women shave their heads to make themselves more beautiful and show off their colourful jewellery. They shave on special occasions with razor blades and a mixture of milk and water.

3

It is the Masai warriors who wear their hair long. They spend several days dressing each other's hair, coating it with a mixture of red soil called ochre and animal fat. They rub the strands together to

make little twisted ropes of hair and gather them together with clips of wood. Masai men often put sweet-smelling leaves under their arms to make them smell nice. They, too, wear lots of jewellery.

Crafts

In many parts of the world people still make the things they need by hand. Some countries are famous for the work done by their craftsmen. Beautiful carpets are made in Iran, fine lace is made in Spain, Morocco is famous for its leather crafts and Indonesia for its silver work. Most craftsmen work with traditional tools and to patterns and designs that have been followed for hundreds of years. Nowadays they sell most of their work to tradesmen.

Weaving

Most cloth is now made in factories by machines, but some craftsmen still use hand looms to weave sheep's wool, goats' hair, cotton and silk into cloth.

1 Baskets

This English man is making a basket with willow sticks. Good baskets cannot be made by machines, so they are still made by hand all over the world.

Mexican women weave brightly coloured cotton cloth for clothes. Weaving is done on looms which hold the long "warp" threads tight while the coloured threads are woven in and out with wooden shuttles. This back-strap loom is easy to pack up and carry around.

Spinning

Cotton and wool must be spun into yarn before they can be woven. This Greek woman is spinning wool on a spindle.

2

Sticks, leaves, grasses and straw can all be woven to make baskets. This Kraho Indian woman from Brazil weaves baskets of palm leaves for carrying fruit.

Carpet making

In Turkey, carpets are made by knotting short pieces of wool on to the upright threads of wall looms. They are made by women and girls working at home. Carpets of different designs and colours are made in different regions.

Dyeing

The yarn is dyed with natural plant colours or chemical dyes. In Morocco, men dye wool in big pits or vats.

Pottery

Pottery is made from clay which is baked until it becomes hard. In many countries, local village potters make clay pots for the villagers to carry water or store food in.

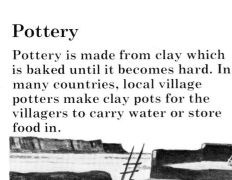

Smooth, even pots are made by shaping the clay while it spins round on a wheel. This Turkish man works as a potter and sells his pots to shops in the towns.

Egyptian women buy huge pots from village potters to carry water from the well. Many of them do not have running water in their homes.

In this pueblo village in the state of New Mexico, U.S.A., an Indian woman is shaping a pot from coils of clay. She smooths the coils together with her fingers. When the pot has been baked, she will paint on it special patterns which have been used in this region for hundreds of years. Villagers and tourists buy the pots.

Batik

In Indonesia, patterns are made on cloth by a special method called *batik*. This woman is painting the pattern with melted wax from a wooden pen. When the cloth is dyed, the colour does not sink into the waxed areas. Later she paints more wax patterns and re-dyes the cloth to make beautiful and intricate patterns.

How to paint wax pictures

You can use the batik method to paint unusual pictures.

1. DRAW PATTERN ON PAPER WITH WHITE CANDLE

2. PAINT PAPER YELLOW

WAXED BITS STAY

SHARPEN CANDLE WITH SCISSORS

3. WHEN DRY, DO SOME MORE WAX PATTERNS

WAX HERE

4. PAINT BLUE ALL OVER

WHITE UNWAXED BITS GO GREEN (YELLOW + BLUE = GREEN)

Carving

Dutch craftsmen still carve wooden clogs by hand. They sell them to tourists as few people in Holland now wear clogs.

The wood carvings from West Africa are famous. This bird was carved by one of the Ashanti people, who live in Ghana.

Bark painting

Australian Aboriginals are well-known for the paintings they do on bark from eucalyptus trees. This is a painting of a kangaroo.

Beliefs

People round the world have different beliefs and belong to different religions. On pages 84–87, you can find out about the main world religions followed by people from many different countries.*

Tribal peoples have their own religions and beliefs. As they are giving up their traditional ways of life, however, they are also changing their beliefs. Many tribal peoples now belong to one of the world religions, such as Christianity or Islam.

1 These flute players in the Amazon jungle pray to their gods with music. They are asking them to end the rainy season so they can start fishing again.

2 This Aboriginal man from Australia is doing a wind dance. The rustle of the leaves tied to his legs makes a sound like the wind which he hopes will bring fish to the shore.

Frightening off spirits

3 The Ho people in eastern India believe in spirits which live in plants. This priest is thanking the spirit of the harvest for protecting the crop, by offering it a cock.

4 Villagers in Nigeria leave food for the spirits of their ancestors at this shrine. They believe the spirits will bring bad luck if they are not looked after.

5 Some Chinese, especially in Hong Kong, believe that their ancestral spirits protect them. In return they offer food and burn incense at their graves.

Witchcraft

In this street market in South Africa you can buy medicines to keep away witches. Many tribal peoples in Africa believe that illness and misfortune can be caused by witches' spells.

This man from the Ivory Coast is a witch-finder. He looks into a bowl of water and sees the faces of witches who have put spells on people.

The magic things in this Angolan man's bowl help him to find witches. He shakes them and reads answers in the way they fall.

Some witch-finders use rubbing boards like this. They ask questions and slide the knob along the board. When it sticks, they know the answers.

*The chart on pages 28-31 shows the religions practised in each country.

Mask to frighten spirits.

Mask to hide person

Mask that looks like a bird.

For special ceremonies and dances, tribal peoples often wear masks. Sometimes these are to hide them from evil spirits, or frighten off dangerous ghosts. Other masks are worn so that people can talk to spirits without being recognized.

Ideas for making masks

Here are some ideas for making masks.

CARDBOARD MASK

1. CUT A PIECE OF CARD TO COVER YOUR FACE

EYE HOLES

STRING HOLES

MOUTH HOLE

2. PAINT AND DECORATE MASK

FEATHERS OR LEAVES

PAPER TONGUE GLUED ON TO MASK

DRINKING STRAW MASK

STRING HOLES

BEND 10cm FROM END

EYE HOLES

BEND

1. CUT A STRIP OF CARD 50cm LONG, 10cm WIDE

LONG STRAWS

STRING

CUT STRAWS TO FIT

2. STICK STRAWS ON WITH STICKY TAPE

Useful things for decorating masks: string, wool, raffia, paints, bottle tops, silver paper, feathers.

By the light of a full moon, these Karaja Indians from Brazil dance through their village dressed in coconut fibre and grasses. They stamp their feet and shake rattles to frighten away evil spirits.

The evil eye

Some people believe that sickness and bad luck can be caused by people looking at them with the "evil eye". To protect themselves they wear charms. People round the world have different superstitions. In Britain, horseshoes are believed to bring good luck.

1 Blue beads, like those on the harness of this Greek bull, are supposed to ward off the evil eye. Silver charms shaped like hands are also supposed to give protection.

2 Fishermen in Portugal paint eyes on their boats. They are said to help them catch a lot of fish because the eyes can "see" where the fish are.

3 This Nuba girl from the Sudan, in Africa, wears special herbs in pouches round her neck. These keep away evil spirits and help to bring her good luck.

World religions

Judaism

Judaism is the religion of the Jewish people. There are about 12 million Jews. Over three million of them live in Israel, where Judaism began over 3,000 years ago.

Jews believe that there is one God and that they have a special duty to worship him. They believe that they are descended from a tribe of people called the Hebrews, and that God chose two of the Hebrew people, Abraham and Moses, to be his messengers.

Jews believe that God gave Moses the Ten Commandments, written on stone tablets. The Commandments are rules saying how people should live together and worship God.

This Rabbi, or Jewish teacher, is reading from the Jews' most holy book, called the Torah. The Torah is written by hand in the Hebrew language and Jews believe it contains God's words to Moses.

The Sabbath is a holy day for Jews. It begins on Friday at sunset, when Jewish families eat a special Sabbath meal and light the Sabbath candles. It ends when it gets dark on Saturday.

On the Sabbath Jews worship God in the synagogue. When boys are 13 and girls are 12 they should begin to live by the Jewish traditions. This is called the age of Bar-mitzvah.

This is the Western Wall in Jerusalem where Jews go to pray. It is the remains of an ancient temple which was destroyed over 2,000 years ago and is a very holy place for Jews.

Christianity

Christians believe that a man called Jesus Christ, born nearly 2,000 years ago, was the son of God.

When Jesus was born, some Jews believed he was the "Messiah", sent from God to bring peace on Earth. They became the first Christians. Followers of Jesus spread his teachings across the world and today, nearly a quarter of all the people in the world is Christian.

The life of Jesus is described in the New Testament, part of a book called the Bible which is holy to Christians. Jesus spent his life teaching about God and healing people. He chose 12 followers, or disciples, to be with him and carry on his work. Christians also believe, like Jews, that Abraham and Moses were messengers of God.

Islam

People who follow the religion of Islam are called Muslims. They believe there is one God whom they call Allah, and that the Prophet Muhammad, who was born 1,400 years ago in Mecca, Arabia, was the messenger of God. Muslims believe that Abraham, Moses and Jesus were also God's messengers. The followers of Muhammad spread the ideas of Islam through the Middle East. Today it is the main religion of all the Arab countries, and also of Pakistan and parts of Africa and South-East Asia.

Minaret—the tall tower of a mosque.

Religious symbols

The Star of David, king of the Jews in Bible times, and the Menorah, a special candlestick, are Jewish symbols.

The cross is a Christian symbol. It can be seen in churches and shrines, by roadsides and in stained glass windows.

| Turkey | Algeria | Pakistan |

The crescent shape of a new moon is the symbol of Islam. Flags of many Muslim countries have crescents and stars on them.

The Muslim holy book is called the Koran. Muslims believe the Koran is an account of God's words to Muhammad and it is always written in Arabic. This is a page from a very old Koran.

From the tall tower of a mosque, a man calls Muslims to prayer. They are supposed to pray five times a day. Before they go in to a mosque they should take off their shoes and wash.

If they are not near a mosque, Muslims can spread out prayer mats and say their prayers. They turn to face in the direction of the city of Mecca and recite from the Koran.

Building called the Kaaba.

Mecca is a holy place for Muslims. Once in their lives, if they can, they are supposed to make a pilgrimage to the city. There, they pray at the holy building called the Kaaba.

Jesus died by being crucified, which means he was nailed to a cross. In his lifetime he was loved and followed by many people, but some of the Jews feared his power.

Christians believe that Jesus rose from the dead and now lives with God in heaven. They believe that if they lead good lives, they too will go to heaven when they die.

On Sundays, Christians go to church to worship God. This picture shows the church of the Holy Sepulchre in Jerusalem which traditionally marks the place where Jesus was buried.

When people become Christians they promise to try and follow Jesus and are baptized. Most Christians are baptized when they are babies and their godparents make the promise for them.

21

Hinduism

Hinduism began about 4,000 years ago and is the oldest world religion. There are about 500 million Hindus, most of whom live in India.

Hindus believe in reincarnation, that is, they believe that when people die, they are born again into other bodies until they are good enough to be united with God. If people lead bad lives, they believe they may be reborn as animals.

Buddhism

Buddhism was started in India about 2,500 years ago by a man called Gautama who is known as the Buddha. He taught that suffering is caused by people's selfish behaviour and that if they try to lead good lives they will be happy and have peace of mind. Buddhists believe that they are born again and again into this world, until they reach Nirvana, a state of everlasting peace.

1 This is a statue of a Hindu god called Shiva, Lord of Dance. Hindus worship many gods and goddesses but they believe that each one represents a form of the highest God.

2 Hindus often have shrines in their homes, where they worship their gods. They pray and light candles at the shrines, make offerings of food and read stories about the gods from their holy books.

This is a golden statue of Buddha in front of which Buddhists meditate about his teachings. He wanted to be thought of as a guide and not as an idol to be worshipped.

To help them lead better lives and move nearer to Nirvana, Buddhists visit shrines where they make offerings of food and flowers and meditate on Buddha's teachings.

3 The River Ganges is a very sacred place for Hindus and they make pilgrimages to it. They wash away their sins in the water and float trays of flowers and incense on the river as offerings to the gods.

Many Buddhist men live in monasteries for a few weeks and some spend their lives as monks. They shave their heads, wear yellow robes and carry begging bowls for food. They lead very simple lives and spend much time meditating. They also teach children about Buddhism and take care of funerals and other ceremonies. Buddhists believe that if they try and follow the example of the monks, it will help them reach Nirvana.

This wheel carved in stone is a Buddhist symbol. The eight spokes stand for the main points of Buddha's teachings.

4

When Hindus die their bodies are burned and the ashes are sprinkled in rivers. Their families pray that their souls will find their way to God and not be reborn again into this world.

5

Hindus have great respect for animals because they believe that everything has a soul. Cows are specially sacred and are allowed to wander freely in the streets.

Sikhism

This religion was begun by Guru Nanak, a spiritual leader who lived in India about 500 years ago. He taught that the caste system was wrong and that people should worship only one god. Today there are about 12 million Sikhs.

Sikhs worship God in their temples and read from the Granth, their holy book which contains the teachings of their leaders or "Gurus".

The caste system

Every Hindu is born into a group called a caste. Some of the castes are thought to be higher and purer than others and priests come from the highest caste.

One of the most important Hindu duties is to obey caste rules. Different castes are supposed to do different work and they are not supposed to marry people from other castes.

Some people in India think the caste system is unfair and are trying to change it.

This man is a shoemaker and he is a member of one of the lowest castes, called the Harijans. Hindus believe that if they obey caste rules they may be reborn into higher castes.

Sikh men and women are not supposed to cut their hair. The men wear turbans to keep it in place and silver bangles on their wrists.

Map of world religions

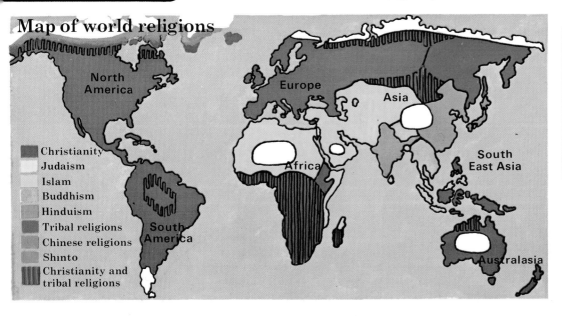

North America

Europe

Asia

Africa

South East Asia

South America

Australasia

Christianity
Judaism
Islam
Buddhism
Hinduism
Tribal religions
Chinese religions
Shinto
Christianity and tribal religions

Shinto

Shinto is an ancient religion which is practised in Japan. People worship spirits at shrines where they hang prayer notes and offer food and money.

23

Celebrations and festivals

All round the world, festivals are times when people dress up in their best clothes, eat special food and give presents.

In most countries, the main festivals celebrate special events in people's religions, such as the birth of a prophet. Other celebrations mark the coming of the new year, or special days such as birthdays.

Christmas

Every year on 25 December, Christians celebrate Christmas to remember the birth of Jesus Christ. Christians in different countries have their own special customs which take place during the Christmas season. Many have stories about St Nicholas, known as Santa Claus, who brings presents.

1 Holland

On 6 December, St Nicholas' Day, Santa Claus fills children's shoes with presents and takes the straw and carrots they leave for his horse.

2 Italy

Lady Befana brings gifts on 6 January. Legend says she was too busy to visit Jesus when he was born, so now she looks for him at every house.

3 Austria

People dress up in masks and straw to tease children. They pretend to be the companions of St Nicholas who used to punish naughty children.

4 Sweden

Early in the morning on St Lucia's day, 13 December, young girls wearing crowns of candles offer people special wheat cakes.

5 Mexico

Christmas decorations called pinatas are full of sweets and nuts. Children are blindfolded and have to try and break the pinatas with sticks.

Buddha's birthday

This Burmese girl is lighting candles to honour Buddha's birthday. Buddhists also celebrate the day a man becomes a monk.

New Year

New Year is celebrated on different days around the world because people use different systems to work out their calendars. In some countries the New Year begins on a different day each year.

Many New Year customs probably began as ways of chasing away the evil spirits of the old year and welcoming good fortune.

In parts of India, the Hindu New Year is marked by the Diwali festival. Patterns of rice flour on doorsteps welcome the goddess of wealth.

Chinese people all over the world celebrate their New Year with dragon dances and firecrackers to frighten away evil spirits.

Hindu festivals

There are many festivals in India as Hindus have lots of gods to honour. This is the "Car" festival for the god Juggernaut*, Lord of the Universe. Huge carts with statues of the god, attended by priests, are pulled through the streets.

Weddings

At Greek weddings, after the church ceremony, it is the custom for guests to pin paper money on the bride and bridegroom.

Arab Muslim marriages usually take place at home. A marriage contract is signed and then there is a party for relatives and friends.

In Hindu marriage ceremonies, the couple are joined with a white cloth. Parents usually choose whom their children should marry.

For Shinto weddings in Japan, the bride often wears a kimono and changes into modern clothes for the reception.

Jewish festivals

Jews celebrate many events believed to have happened in their history. The Passover festival reminds them of when Moses rescued their ancestors, the Israelites, from slavery over 3,000 years ago. The Israelites had to escape quickly and did not have time to let their bread rise. To remind them of this, Jews eat flat, unleavened bread, during Passover week.

For the Sukkot festival, people build little huts in their gardens. This reminds them of how their ancestors lived in the wilderness.

Muslim feast

During the month of Ramadan, Muslims are supposed to fast. They may not eat or drink during daylight hours. At the end of the month they feast and give presents.

May Day

Under the Soviet Union, soldiers and people with red flags used to march through Red Square in Moscow on 1 May every year. They were celebrating May Day, a communist holiday.

How to make a pinata

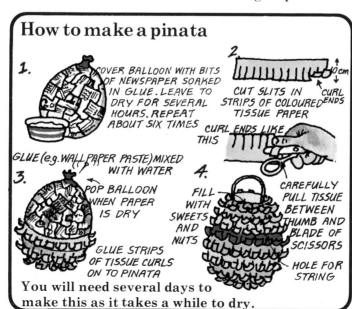

1. COVER BALLOON WITH BITS OF NEWSPAPER SOAKED IN GLUE. LEAVE TO DRY FOR SEVERAL HOURS. REPEAT ABOUT SIX TIMES

GLUE (e.g. WALLPAPER PASTE) MIXED WITH WATER

2. CUT SLITS IN STRIPS OF COLOURED TISSUE PAPER   CURL ENDS   0cm

CURL ENDS LIKE THIS

3. POP BALLOON WHEN PAPER IS DRY

GLUE STRIPS OF TISSUE CURLS ON TO PINATA

4. FILL WITH SWEETS AND NUTS   CAREFULLY PULL TISSUE BETWEEN THUMB AND BLADE OF SCISSORS   HOLE FOR STRING

You will need several days to make this as it takes a while to dry.

*This is the origin of our word juggernaut, meaning large truck.

Music and dancing

In the past, people in Europe and America danced their traditional folk dances at fairs, festivals, weddings and celebrations. Folk dances are very old and the steps have been passed down from parents to children for hundreds of years. Nowadays they are mostly performed by dance groups in national costumes.

In other parts of the world, people have traditional dances which they perform at festivals or use to tell stories of their gods and heroes.

Balinese dancers

The flamenco dances of southern Spain are usually danced by gypsies to the music of guitars. They wear frilly skirts and make clicking sounds with castanets.

In Russian Cossack dancing, the men do somersaults and high kicks to show their skill. These dances were first done by Cossack soldiers several hundred years ago.

In India, Hindus worship their gods with dances. They use movements of their hands and eyes to tell stories about the gods.

On the island of Bali, in Indonesia, dancers act out stories about their Hindu gods with intricate movements of their eyes and bodies. Before the dances, which are often performed in temples, offerings of fruit and flowers are made to the gods. The dancers wear richly coloured silk costumes and head-dresses.

Balinese children begin to learn to dance when they are about six years old. It takes years of training to master the movements.

The dancers need perfect muscle control to perform the delicate hand and arm movements, all of which have special meanings.

This dancer is dressed up as the wicked witch, Rangda. Many of the dances are stories about the triumph of good over evil.

Musical instruments

Each region of the world has its own folk music which is played on traditional musical instruments to accompany folk dances.

The Spanish guitar probably developed from instruments like the Arabic "ud", shown on the right.

The Arabic ud is a kind of lute which is played by plucking the strings. It is used in classical and folk music.

The sitar is an Indian instrument which has six or seven strings. The person playing it sits on the floor and plucks the strings with their fingers.

Bagpipes are played to accompany Scottish sword dances. Air from the bag is forced through the pipes to make sounds.

In Indonesia, xylophones, gongs, bamboo pipes and drums are played in village orchestras.

Drums are often played in African music. Here they are being heated so that they make the right sounds.

4 Japanese Kabuki plays are a mixture of mime, music and dance. People offstage chant stories about ancient heroes and the actors wear traditional costume.

5 These Zulu men in South Africa are doing a warrior dance. In the past these were performed before battles, but now Zulus do them for tourists.

6 The Maori people of New Zealand dress up in their traditional clothes and dance on special occasions. Many of the dances tell stories of the Maoris' past.

Peoples of the world chart

PEOPLE	WHERE THEY LIVE	LANGUAGE	RELIGION	CURRENCY
Afghans	Afghanistan	Dari Persian, Pushtu	Muslim	Afghani (100 puls)
Albanians	Albania	Albanian	Muslim, Christian	Lek (100 qintars)
Algerians	Algeria	Arabic, Berber, French	Muslim	Dinar (100 centimes)
Americans	United States of America	English, Spanish	Christian, Jewish, Muslim	U.S. dollar (100 cents)
Andorrans	Andorra	Spanish, French, Catalan	Christian	French franc and Spanish peseta
Angolans	Angola	Portuguese, Bantu languages	Christian, tribal religions	Angolan kwanza (100 centavos)
Arabs	Egypt, Syria, Jordan, Kuwait, United Arab Emirates, Oman, Saudi Arabia, Lebanon, Israel, Qatar, Bahrain, Libya, Tunisia, Algeria, Morocco, Yemen	Arabic	Muslim, Christian	Money of countries where they live
Argentinians	Argentina	Spanish	Christian	Argentinian peso
Australians	Australia	English	Christian	Australian dollar (100 cents)
Austrians	Austria	German	Christian	Schilling (100 groschen)
Bahamians	Bahamas	English	Christian	Bahamian dollar
Bahrainis	Bahrain	Arabic, English	Muslim, Christian	Bahraini dinar
Bamar	Myanmar	Bamar, English	Buddhist, Muslim, Hindu, tribal religions	Kyat (100 pyas)
Bangladeshis	Bangladesh	Bengali, Hindi, Bihari, English	Muslim, Hindu, Christian, Buddhist	Taka (100 paisa)
Barbadians	Barbados	English, Bajan	Christian	Barbados dollar
Belgians	Belgium	French, Flemish, German	Christian	Belgian franc (100 cents)
Belize, citizens of	Belize	English, American Indian languages	Christian	Belizean dollar (100 cents)
Beninese	Benin	French, Fon, Adja, Bariba, Yoruba	Tribal religions, Christian, Muslim	African financial community franc
Bhutanese	Bhutan	Dzongkha (a Tibetan dialect)	Buddhist, Hindu	Ngultrum (100 chetrum)
Bolivians	Bolivia	Spanish, American Indian languages	Christian, tribal religions	Bolivian peso (100 centavos)

PEOPLE	WHERE THEY LIVE	LANGUAGE	RELIGION	CURRENCY
Bosnians	Bosnia-Herzegovina	Serbo-Croat	Christian, Muslim	Dinar (100 para)
Botswanans	Botswana	Se-Tswana, English	Christian, tribal religions	Pula
Brazilians	Brazil	Portuguese, American Indian languages	Christian, tribal religions	Cruzeiro (100 centavos)
British	United Kingdom	English, Welsh, Gaelic	Christian	Pound sterling (100 pence)
Bruneians	Brunei	Malay, Chinese, English	Muslim, Buddhist, Chinese religions	Bruneian dollar (100 cents)
Bulgarians	Bulgaria	Bulgarian, Turkish, Macedonian	Christian, Muslim	Lev (100 stotinki)
Burkina Faso, citizens of	Burkina Faso	French, Mossi	Tribal religions, Muslim, Christian	African financial community franc
Burundi, citizens of	Burundi	French, Swahili, Kirundi	Christian and tribal religions	Burundi franc
Cambodians	Cambodia	Khmer, French	Buddhist	Riel (100 sen)
Cameroonians	Cameroon	French, English, African languages	Tribal religions, Christian, Muslim	African financial community franc
Canadians	Canada	English, French	Christian	Canadian dollar (100 cents)
Cape Verdeans	Cape Verde Islands	Portuguese, Creole	Christian	Cape Verde escudo
Central African Republic, citizens of	Central African Republic	Sangho, French	Christian, tribal religions	African financial community franc
Chad, citizens of	Chad	French, Arabic, African languages	Muslim, Christian, tribal religions	African financial community franc
Chileans	Chile	Spanish	Christian	Chilean peso
Chinese	China, Taiwan, Hong Kong	Mandarin, other Chinese languages English	Buddhist, Chinese religions, Christian, Muslim	Yuan (100 fen), New Taiwan dollar, Hong Kong dollar
Colombians	Colombia	Spanish	Christian	Colombian peso
Comorians	Comoros	French, Arabic, Comoran	Muslim, Christian	Comoro franc
Congolese	Congo	French, Bantu languages	Tribal religions, Christian, Muslim	African financial community franc
Costa Ricans	Costa Rica	Spanish	Christian	Costa Rica colon
Croatians	Croatia	Serbo-Croat	Christian, Muslim	Dinar (100 para)
Cubans	Cuba	Spanish, English	Christian	Cuban peso

PEOPLE	WHERE THEY LIVE	LANGUAGE	RELIGION	CURRENCY
Cypriots	Cyprus	Greek, Turkish, English	Christian, Muslim	Cyprus pound, Turkish lira
Czechs	Czech Republic	Czech, Slovak,	Christian	Koruna (100 haleru)
Danes	Denmark	Danish	Muslim, Christian	Danish Krone (100 øre)
Djiboutians	Djibouti	French, African languages	Muslim, Christian	Djibouti franc
Dominicans	Dominican Republic	Spanish	Christian	Dominican peso
Dutch	Netherlands	Dutch	Christian	Guilder (100 cents)
Ecuadoreans	Ecuador	Spanish	Christian	Sucre (100 centavos)
Egyptians	Egypt	Arabic, English, French	Muslim, Christian	Egyptian pound (100 piastres)
Equatorial Guineans	Equatorial Guinea	Spanish, Fang, Bubi	Muslim, Christian	Ekuele (100 centimos)
English	England	English	Christian	Pound sterling (100 pence)
Eritreans	Eritrea	Amharic, Tigrinya, Arabic, tribal languages	Muslim, Christian	Birr
Ethiopians	Ethiopia	Amharic Arabic, Somali	Muslim, Christian	Ethiopian birr
Fijians	Fiji	English, Fijian, Hindi	Christian, Hindu	Fiji dollar (100 cents)
Filipinos	Philippines	Tagalog, English, local languages	Christian, Muslim, tribal religions	Filipino peso
Finns	Finland	Finnish, Swedish	Christian	Markka (100 pennia)
French	France	French	Christian	French franc (100 centimes)
Gabonese	Gabon	French, Fang, Eshira	Christian, tribal religions	African financial community franc
Gambians	Gambia	English, Mandinka, Fula, Wollof	Muslim, Christian	Dalasi (100 butut)
Germans	Germany	German	Christian	Deutschmark (100 pfennige)
Ghanaians	Ghana	English, African languages	Christian, Muslim, tribal religions	New cedi (100 pesewas)
Gibraltar, people of	Gibraltar	English, Spanish	Christian,	Gibraltar pound
Greeks	Greece	Greek	Christian	Drachma (100 leptae)
Grenadians	Grenada	English, French, patois	Christian	East Caribbean dollar

PEOPLE	WHERE THEY LIVE	LANGUAGE	RELIGION	CURRENCY
Guatemalans	Guatemala	Spanish, American Indian languages	Christian	Quetzal (100 centavos)
Guineans	Guinea	French, Fulani, Susu, Malinke	Muslim, tribal religions	Syli (100 cauris)
Guinea-Bissauans	Guinea-Bissau	Portuguese, Creole, Balante, Fulani, Malinke	Tribal religions, Muslim	Guinean peso (100 centavos)
Guyanese	Guyana	English, Hindi, Urdu	Christian, Hindu, Muslim	Guyanese dollar
Haitians	Haiti	Creole, French	Christian, Voodoo	Gourde (100 centimes)
Hondurans	Honduras	Spanish, American Indian languages	Christian	Lempira (100 centavos)
Hungarians	Hungary	Magyar	Christian	Forint (100 filler)
Icelanders	Iceland	Icelandic	Christian	Icelandic krona
Indians	India	Hindu and 15 other main languages	Hindu, Muslim, Christian, Sikh, Buddhist	Rupee (100 paisa)
Indonesians	Indonesia	Basha, Indonesian, Javanese, Madurese, Sundanese	Muslim, Christian, Buddhist, Hindu	Rupiah (100 sen)
Iranians	Iran	Farsi, Arabic, Baluchi	Muslim, Christian	Iranian rial (100 dinars)
Iraqis	Iraq	Arabic, Kurdish,	Muslim, Christian	Iraqi dinar
Irish	Ireland	English, Gaelic	Christian	Irish pound (100 pence)
Israelis	Israel	Hebrew, Arabic, Yiddish	Jewish, Muslim	Israeli pound (100 agorot)
Italians	Italy	Italian	Christian	Italian lira
Ivory Coast, citizens of	Ivory Coast	African languages, French	Tribal religions, Muslim, Christian	African financial community franc
Jamaicans	Jamaica	English, patois	Christian, Rastafarian	Jamaican dollar
Japanese	Japan	Japanese	Buddhist, Shintoist	Yen (100 sen)
Jews	Israel and other countries	Hebrew, Yiddish or languages of countries where they live	Jewish	Money of the countries where they live
Jordanians	Jordan	Arabic	Muslim, Christian	Jordanian dinar
Kenyans	Kenya	English, Swahili, Kikuyu, Luo	Christian, Muslim, tribal religions,	Kenyan shilling (100 cents)
Koreans	North Korea, South Korea	Korean	Buddhist, Chinese religions, Christian	Won (100 jeon)

PEOPLE	WHERE THEY LIVE	LANGUAGE	RELIGION	CURRENCY
Kuwaitis	Kuwait	Arabic, English	Muslim, Christian	Kuwaiti dinar
Lao	Laos	Lao, French, English	Buddhist, tribal religions	Liberation kip (100 at)
Lebanese	Lebanon	Arabic, French, English	Christian, Muslim	Lebanese pound (100 piastres)
Leeward Islanders	St Kitts-Nevis, Antigua and Barbuda	English	Christian	East Caribbean dollar
Lesotho, citizens of	Lesotho	Sesotho, English	Christian	Maluti
Liberians	Liberia	English, African languages	Christian, Muslim	Liberian dollar (100 cents)
Libyans	Libya	Arabic	Muslim	Libyan dinar
Liechtenstein, citizens of	Liechtenstein	German	Christian	Swiss franc
Luxembourg, citizens of	Luxembourg	Letzeburgesch, French, German	Christian	Luxembourg franc (100 centimes)
Madagascans	Madagascar	Malagasy, French	Tribal religions, Christian, Muslim	Madagascan franc
Malawians	Malawi	Nyanja, English, Chichewa	Tribal religions, Christian	Malawi kwacha (100 tambala)
Malaysians	Malaysia	Malay, English, Chinese, Indian languages	Muslim, Buddhist, Hindu, Christian	Ringgit (100 sen)
Maldivians	Maldives	Divehi	Muslim	Rufiyaa
Malians	Mali	Bambara, French	Muslim, tribal religions	Malian franc
Maltese	Malta	Maltese, Engllish, Italian	Christian	Maltese lira
Mauritanians	Mauritania	French, Arabic	Muslim	Ouguiya (5 khoums)
Mauritians	Mauritius	English, French, Creole, Hindi, Urdu	Hindu, Christian, Muslim	Mauritian rupee (100 cents)
Mexicans	Mexico	Spanish	Christian	Mexican peso (100 centavos)
Monégasque	Monaco	French	Christian	French franc
Mongolians	Mongolia	Khalkha, Mongolian, Russian	Buddhist	Tugrik (100 mongo)
Moroccans	Morocco	Arabic, Berber	Muslim, Christian	Dirham (100 centimes)
Mozambicans	Mozambique	Portuguese, African languages	Tribal religions, Christian Muslim	Metical
Namibians	Namibia	Afrikaans, English, African languages	Christian, tribal religions	South African rand
Nauruans	Nauru	Nauruan, English	Christian	Australian dollar
Nepalese	Nepal	Nepali, Maithir, Bhojpuri	Hindu, Buddhist Muslim	Nepalese rupee (100 paisa)

PEOPLE	WHERE THEY LIVE	LANGUAGE	RELIGION	CURRENCY
New Zealanders	New Zealand	English, Maori	Christian	New Zealand dollar
Nicaraguans	Nicaragua	Spanish	Christian	Cordoba-oro
Niger, citizens of	Niger	French, African languages	Muslim, Christian, tribal religions	African financial community franc
Nigerians	Nigeria	English, Hausa, Ibo, Yoruba	Muslim, Christian tribal religions	Naira (100 kobo)
Norwegians	Norway	Norwegian, Lapp	Christian	Norwegian krone (100 øre)
Omanis	Oman	Arabic	Muslim	Omani rial
Pakistanis	Pakistan	Punjabi, Urdu, Sindhi, Pushtu	Muslim, Hindu, Christian	Pakistani rupee (100 paisa)
Panamanians	Panama	Spanish, English	Christian	Balboa (100 centesimos)
Papua New Guineans	Papua New Guinea	English, Pidgin, Moru	Christian tribal religions	Kina (100 toea)
Paraguayans	Paraguay	Spanish, American Indian languages	Christian, tribal religions	Guarani (100 centimos)
Peruvians	Peru	Spanish, American Indian lanuages: Quechua, Aymara	Christian, tribal religions	Peruvian sol (100 centavos)
Poles	Poland	Polish	Christian	Zloty (100 groszy)
Portuguese	Portugal	Portuguese	Christian	Portugese escudo (100 centavos)
Qatar, citizens of	Qatar	Arabic, English	Muslim	Qatar riyal (100 dirhams)
Romanians	Romania	Romanian, Magyar, German	Christian	Leu (100 bani)
Rwandese	Rwanda	French, Kinyarwanda, Kiswahili	Christian, Muslim, tribal religions	Rwandan franc (100 centimes)
Salvadoreans	El Salvador	Spanish	Christian	Colón (100 centavos)
San Marino, citizens of	San Marino	Italian	Christian	Italian lira
São Tomé and Princípe, citizens of	São Tomé and Princípe	Portuguese	Christian	Dobra
Saudi Arabians	Saudi Arabia	Arabic	Muslim	Saudi riyal (100 halalah)
Scots	Scotland	English, Gaelic	Christian	Pound sterling
Senegalese	Senegal	French, Wolof	Muslim, Christian, tribal reliigions	African financial community franc
Seychellois	Seychelles	Creole, English, French	Christian	Seychellois rupee
Sierra Leoneans	Sierra Leone	English, Krio, Mende, Temne	Tribal religions, Muslim, Christian	Leone (100 cents)
Singaporeans	Singapore	Malay, Mandarin, Chinese, Tamil, English	Muslim, Buddhist, Hindu, Taoist, Christian	Singaporean dollar (100 cents)

PEOPLE	WHERE THEY LIVE	LANGUAGE	RELIGION	CURRENCY
Slovaks	Slovakia	Slovak, Czech, Magyar	Christian	Koruna (100 haleru)
Slovenians	Slovenia	Slovenian	Christian, Muslim	Slovenian dinar (Tolar)
Solomon Islanders	Solomon Islands	Roviana, Marovo	Tribal religions, Christian	Solomon Island dollar
Somalis	Somalia	Somali, Arabic, English, Italian	Muslim, Christian	Somali shilling
South Africans	South Africa	Afrikaans, English, Xhosa, Zulu, Tswana, Sesotho, Sepedi	Christian, Muslim, Hindu, tribal religions	South African rand (100 cents)
Soviet Union former citizens of	Russian Federation Ukraine Uzbekistan Kazakhstan Belarus Azerbaijan Georgia Tajikistan Kyrgyzstan Moldova Lithuania Turkmenistan Armenia Latvia Estonia	Russian Ukrainian Uzbek Kazakh Belorussian Azeri Georgian Tajik Kirghizian Romanian Lithuanian Turkmen Armenian Latvian Estonian	Christian Christian Muslim Muslim Christian Muslim Christian Muslim Muslim Christian Christian Muslim Christian Christian Christian	Rouble Rouble Rouble Rouble Rouble Manat Rouble Rouble Rouble Rouble Lat Rouble Rouble Lat Kroon
Spaniards	Spain	Spanish	Christian	Peseta (100 centimos)
Sri Lankans	Sri Lanka	Sinhala, Tamil, English	Buddhist, Hindu, Christian, Muslim	Sri Lankan rupee (100 cents)
Sudanese	Sudan	Arabic, Nilotic	Muslim, tribal religions	Sudanese pound
Surinamese	Surinam	Dutch, HIndustani, Javanese, Creole	Christian, Hindu, Muslim	Surinamese guilder (100 cents)
Swazis	Swaziland	English, Siswati	Christian, tribal religions	Lilangeni
Swedes	Sweden	Swedish, Finnish, Lapp	Christian	Swedish krona (100 öre)
Swiss	Switzerland	German, French, Italian, Romansh	Christian	Swiss franc (100 centimes)
Syrians	Syria	Arabic	Muslim, Christian	Syrian pound (100 piastres)
Tanzanians	Tanzania	English, Swahili	Christian, Muslim, tribal religions	Tanzanian shilling (100 cents)
Thais	Thailand	Thai	Buddhist, Muslim	Bhat (100 satangs)
Togolese	Togo	French, Ewe, Kabre	Tribal religions, Muslim Christian	African financial community franc

PEOPLE	WHERE THEY LIVE	LANGUAGE	RELIGION	CURRENCY
Tongans	Tonga	Tongan, English	Christian	Pa'anga (100 seniti)
Trinidad and Tobago, citizens of	Trinidad and Tobago	English, Hindu, French, Spanish	Christian, Hindu, Muslim	Trinidad and Tobago dollar (100 cents)
Tunisians	Tunisia	Arabic, French	Muslim, Jewish, Christian	Tunisian dinar
Turks	Turkey	Turkish, Kurdish	Muslim,	Turkish lira (100 kurus)
Ugandans	Uganda	English, Luganda, Ateso, Runyankore	Christian, Muslim, tribal religions	Ugandan shilling (100 cents)
United Arab Emirates, citizens of	United Arab Emirates	Arabic, English	Muslim	United Arab Emirates dirham (100 fils)
Uruguayans	Uruguay	Spanish, American Indian languages	Christian, tribal religions	New Uruguayan peso (100 centesimos)
Vatican City, citizens of	Vatican City	Italian, Latin	Christian	Italian lira
Venezuelans	Venezuela	Spanish	Christian	Bolivar (100 centimos)
Vietnamese	Vietnam	Vietnamese	Buddhist, Chinese religions, Christian	Dong (100 xu)
Welsh	Wales	Welsh, English	Christian	Pound sterling
Western Samoans	Western Samoa	Samoan, English	Christian	Tala (100 sene)
Windward Islanders	Dominica, St Lucia, St Vincent, Grenada	English, French, patois	Christian	East Caribbean dollar
Yemenites	Yemen	Arabic	Muslim	Yemeni rial
Yugoslavs	Fed. Rep. of Yugoslavia	Serbo-Croat, Macedonian	Christian, Muslim	Yugoslav dinar (100 para)
Zairians	Zaire	French, Lingala, Kiswahili, Tshiluba, Kikongo	Tribal religions, Christian	Zaire (100 makuta)
Zambians	Zambia	English, Nyanja, Bemba, Tonga, Lozi, Lunda, Luvale	Christian, tribal religions	Zambian kwacha (100 ngwee)
Zimbabweans	Zimbabwe	English, Sindebele, Shona	Christian, tribal religions	Zimbabwean dollar (100 cents)

Going further

Books to read

Festivals and Customs by Patricia Morrell (Piccolo)
XYZ of Sport by T. Goffe (Transworld)
Sport and Entertainment in Australia by Unstead and Henderson (Black)
The How and Why Book of Costumes by Margaret Smith (Transworld)
Houses and Homes by Carol Bowyer (Usborne)
National Geographic magazine (National Geographic Society) sometimes has good accounts and pictures of people round the world. You can find it in reference libraries and second-hand book shops.

Books about other countries:
Lands and Peoples edited by Kenneth Bailey (Collins)
Macdonald Countries series (Macdonald)
Looking at Other Countries series (Black)

Places to visit

Britain
The Museum of Mankind in London and the Horniman Museum, London have exhibitions about tribal peoples and the Horniman Museum has a good collection of musical instruments from other countries. The Commonwealth Institute in London has exhibitions on all the Commonwealth countries. There are museums with displays about people in Bristol, Brighton, Birmingham, Manchester, Liverpool, Glasgow and Belfast and in the Pitt Rivers Museum in Oxford and the University Museum in Cambridge.

The following museums in Australia, New Zealand and Canada have exhibitions about peoples of the world:
The South Australian Museum, Adelaide, Australia.
Canterbury Museum, Christchurch, New Zealand.
National Museum of Man, Ottawa, Canada; McCord Museum, Montreal, Canada and Royal Ontario Museum, Toronto, Canada.

Index